THE LITTLE SEAGULLS That Didn't Fly

IRIS FAITH

AuthorHouse™ UK
1663 Liberty Drive
Bloomington, IN 47403
www.authorhouse.com
Phone: 1 (800) 839-8640

Published by AuthorHouse 06/29/2018

ISBN: 978-1-5462-8213-6 (sc)
ISBN: 978-1-5462-8214-3 (e)

authorHOUSE®

FOR MY DARLING CHILDREN,
ALL MY LOVE MUM.

The Little Seagulls lived in their nest, with their parents on a Great Tree in CloverDream Forest.

The five little seagulls Ardell, Arty, Vismo, Marty and Mertell were out playing one day in the forest.

When Mr. Parrot and their bird friends were flying past, they asked "Do you all want to come to the party at the castle with us today?"

"No, we don't like walking up the big steep hill to the castle!" replied the little seagulls.
Mr. Parrot and the other birds were puzzled, as they knew seagulls could fly, but they were in a hurry, and flew on!

As the little seagulls walked on, Mrs. Rabbit and her family came hopping up to them. Mrs. Rabbit asked, "Are you all coming to the Castle Party?" "No, it's too far away," the little seagulls replied.

"Okay, see you later," said Mrs. Rabbit, and off they all hopped to the party.

Then The Butterfly Family appeared, as they flew past, they shouted to the little seagulls, "Have you heard about the Castle Party?"

"Yes, and we are not going," the little seagulls quickly replied. The little seagulls were starting to get a little annoyed.

9

Just then their little friends The Tiger Cub and The Fox Cub came racing past. They roared over, "Are you all going to the Party at the Castle? It will be great!"

"No, we are not!" the little seagulls shouted back!

So little tiger and little fox raced on.

The little seagulls were upset, as they really wanted to go to the Castle Party, but they knew they could not walk the long distance to the castle, and be there in time for the party.

The little seagulls were now tired and upset, and they sat down by a tree. Suddenly they heard the hooting of an owl.

As they looked up, there was The Wise Old Owl perched on the branch above them.

"Are you all not going to the Castle Party?" enquired the owl.

"No, we will not be able to get there on time," the little seagulls replied.

"There will be singing, dancing and the most delicious food. Why do you not all fly to the castle?" asked the owl.

"We can't fly!" replied the little seagulls.

"Why do you think that?" enquired the owl

"The wasps told us."

"The wasps said, Seagulls can't fly, that's what they said," explained the little seagulls.
The wise old owl knew that what the wasps had told the little seagulls was wrong, and that the little seagulls could fly, if they just believed that they could.

The owl asked the little seagulls, if they would all like to fly.

"We have always dreamed of being able to fly," sighed the little seagulls.

The wise old owl told the little seagulls that they needed to find five magic coloured eggs. Then the owl instructed the little seagulls that once they found the magic coloured eggs, they each had to throw a magic coloured egg into the air, and catch it, and then The Dream Teacher would appear, and help them to fly.
Then the wise old owl flew off.

The little seagulls shouted after him, "Where do we find the magic coloured eggs?" but the owl was too far away to hear them.

The little seagulls thought to themselves, that they would never be able to find the five magic coloured eggs in the large forest.

Just then the playful little dog, came racing up to the little seagulls. The little dog lived in the house at the edge of the forest. He was out digging in the garden, and had overheard the owl talking to the little seagulls.

The little dog called Rockstar, told the seagulls that he knew where the magic coloured eggs where. He had seen five coloured eggs under a golden bush one day, when he was looking for his lost bone, in an area of Clover Dream Forest called Bright Tree Patch.

The little seagulls told the little dog that, they didn't know where Bright Tree Patch was in the Forest. The little dog told the little seagulls that he would be happy to show them.

So off they all went to find Bright Tree Patch of Clover Dream Forest

The little seagulls followed the little dog for what seemed like hours, till they eventually came to Bright Tree Patch.

BRIGHT
TREE PATCH

The little seagulls were amazed at the size of Bright Tree Patch, and the vast amount of bright coloured bushes in front of them. They were enchanted at the amazing colours of the bushes,but wondered how they would ever find five coloured eggs, in among all those bushes.

The little seagulls and the little dog searched for a very long time. Then just as they were about to give up, the little dog noticed a golden light at the top of the hill.

The little dog shouted to the little seagulls, "Look! There is a golden light! That is where I think the golden bush is!"

They all raced up the hill, and there, where the golden light was, stood an amazing golden bush.

The little dog pulled out from under the bush, a large nest with five coloured eggs in it.

As each little seagull bravely took an egg, threw it up into the air, and caught it again, a great coloured light appeared. From the light a Great Eagle appeared.

The Great Eagle introduced himself to the little seagulls and the little dog. He told them that he was The Dream Teacher the owl had told them about, and that he would help them to fly.

The Great Eagle told the little seagulls to place their coloured eggs in front of them, and start to flap their wings. As they started to flap their wings, the great coloured light appeared again and they started to rise up into the sky. The little seagulls were a bit scared at first, but then after a while they became braver, and gradually started excitedly flying around the sky.

The little seagulls were so excited now as they could fly. They had always dreamed of being able to fly like the other birds.

The little seagulls swooped over the little dog and the eagle, shouting "Thank You!" and off they flew to the castle.

The little seagulls were so happy and thrilled as they excitedly flew to the Castle.

The Wise Old Owl and the Great Eagle knew the little seagulls could fly all along, if they just believed.

The Little Seagulls had a great time at the Castle Party with all their friends. They were eating the most scrumptious food, singing, dancing and telling everyone of their adventure, and of course showing everyone their new flying skills!

The Royal Family of Clover Dream Town presented The Little Seagulls with a great medal, The Star Award, which was only given for great courage and effort. This was given to them as the Great Eagle had told the Royal Family of their courage and efforts in learning to fly.

The Castle Party was now held every year, and the little seagulls performed a great flying display which all of Clover Dream Town and Clover Dream Forest came to see! What a Most Wonderful, Magical and Joyous Land was Clover Dream Forest and Town, a land full of love and joy.

Some of the other animals in Clover Dream Forest displayed their talents at the Castle Party, and some of the people in Clover Dream Town also joined in displaying their talents. Everyone had lots of fun and had a great time at the Castle Party.

THE END

FOR MY DARLING CHILDREN,
MY DARLING CHILDREN, ARE MY LIFE, MY WORLD
AND MY INSPIRATION, ALL MY LOVE MUM.

GOD BLESS YOUS ALWAYS.

CHILDREN AND EVERYONE.....FOLLOW YOUR DREAMS, HAVE FUN.......AND ALWAYS REMEMBER TO FLY WITH YOUR DREAMS.....LOVE I FAITH

Printed in the United States
By Bookmasters

Printed in the United States
By Bookmasters